WRONG

A Novel

POULI VOX

The moral right of the author has been asserted

All rights reserved—Pouli Vox

No part of this publication may be reproduced, stored in a retrieval system or transmitted in any form or by any means, without the prior permission in writing of the publisher, nor be otherwise circulated in any form of binding or cover other than that in which it is published and without a similar condition including this condition being imposed on the subsequent purchaser.

The Empire Publishers publishing
12808 West Airport Blvd Suite 270M Sugar Land, TX 77478
https://empirepublishers.co/about-us
Our books may be purchased in bulk for promotional, educational, or business use. Please contact The Empire Publishers at +(844) 636-4576, or by email at support@theempirepublishers.com

First Edition October 2024

Some Americans drive trucks,
Some Americans write books.

Author's Note

I've only ever cried twice out of a feeling of nationalism.

The first time happened while watching a biracial Miss USA win the Miss Universe pageant. I remember getting choked up and a few tears escaping onto my teenage cheeks. I was sincerely so proud of us. Even then, I felt that this was something that, as a country, we should be proud of. Looking at her in the won tiara, I thought, my teenage sense of justice and idealism full of hope: "America is the BEST." I felt it, and I believed it.

The second round of tears came years and years later. Trump won. This time, confusion replaced pride. *He* was chosen to represent our country? It was shocking. A man so immoral, so dishonest, so gross—couldn't we all see that? How did this happen?

This book honors the longstanding tradition of citizens using humor to taunt and challenge leaders they see as corrupt. While we may lack direct authority, we do possess a formidable strength—the power of the people.

Pouli Vox

Table of Contents

PROLOGUE: ARRIVAL 1

CHAPTER 1: THE ROMANCE 7

CHAPTER 2: THE ROMAN EMPIRE 19

CHAPTER 3: CONSPIRACY 35

CHAPTER 4: PREPPING 44

CHAPTER 5: PULLING THREADS 54

CHAPTER 6: CARNAGE 64

CHAPTER 7: THREE KILLERS, ONE TARGET 74

CHAPTER 8: CHEW 86

CHAPTER 9: WRONG 95

CHAPTER 10: MUNGER 105

CHAPTER 11: THE RESULTS ARE IN 112

EPILOGUE: EVIDENCE 118

PROLOGUE

ARRIVAL

The gleaming jet touched down at McCarran International Airport, its fuselage emblazoned with gold letters spelling TRUMP. As the stairs lowered to the burning tarmac, the Nevada heat shimmered above the heads of waiting reporters and supporters. It was a remarkably hot day, even by Las Vegas standards, enough for some of the sweating reporters to ask themselves whether the job was worth the perspiring armpits and potential heat stroke. The air itself seemed to waver, as if unsure whether to welcome or repel the incoming spectacle.

Then, he emerged: Donald Trump himself, his signature coiffure barely ruffled by the hot breeze. Small, beady eyes squinted as he raised a hand, waving to the crowd with the practiced, mistaken ease of a man who believes the world revolves around him. His suit, damp from the sweltering heat, was anything but impeccably pressed. Behind him, his decidedly better half, Melania Trump, appeared in a black Ralph Lauren coat, despite the heat. Her bored expression was barely hidden behind her designer sunglasses; she looked like a reluctant supporting actor in a B-movie about political ambition gone awry.

"Mr. Trump! Mr. Trump!" shouted a reporter, his voice cracking slightly from the dry heat. "Are you looking forward to the Heart Attack Café fundraiser this evening?"

Trump's eyes lit up, the slightly tangerine wrinkles
around his eyes crinkling like a plastic bin left too long in the sun. "It's going to be tremendous. You know, I've always said, if you're going to have a heart attack, have it in style. And let me tell you: nobody does style like Trump."

His advisor—also beady-eyed and paunchy, a rather flushed-looking man who seemed to be melting in real-time—leaned in, whispering urgently. His whisper was more of a strained hiss, like a tire slowly losing air. "Sir, remember, we're here for serious campaigning and fundraising.

WRONG

The burger thing's just a publicity stunt. This campaign stop in Las Vegas is crucial for your White House bid."

Trump nodded sagely as he leaned back toward his advisor, his expression reminiscent of a toddler pretending to understand quantum physics. "Right, right. Very serious. Did I ever tell you about the time I single-handedly saved Atlantic City's economy with my casinos? The folks here in Atlantic City, they know me. They love Trump. I've got a feeling the wealthy in this town are just itching to support a winner like me."

The advisor's face contorted into a mixture of confusion and resignation, a look that suggested this was far from the first time he'd had to correct his boss's geography. "Uh, sir... we're in Las Vegas."

Trump's face remained impassive, as if the distinction between two entirely different cities was a mere trifle not worth acknowledging. "That's what I said. Vegas, Atlantic City—all the same. Big buildings, lots of gold. Trump gold—the best gold. And soon, we'll have that beautiful gold all over the White House, believe me."

Pouli Vox

Now, they made their way to the waiting limousine, which was less a vehicle and more a small, mobile fortress masquerading as a luxury car. It gleamed with a polished bravado that seemed to imply, "Yes, I'm not yet so important, so I must be compensating for something." The heat radiating off its black exterior was intense enough to fry an egg, or perhaps a political career.

As her husband marched ahead, already waving to imaginary crowds, Melania hung back, her face still hidden behind oversized sunglasses that gleamed with the slightest touch of burnished bronze. A young aide approached her tentatively, noticing the displeased curl of her lip.
"Mrs. Trump, are you ready for the campaign stop? The high-rollers are eager to meet you both." Melania's expression remained unchanged

as
she replied in a low voice, her accent thicker than usual, as if the heat had melted away some of her carefully cultivated Americanisms. "Let's just get this over with. I didn't sign up for politics."

WRONG

The aide, sensing the tension, tried to lighten the mood. "Mrs. Trump? Is everything alright?"

Melania's lips curved further, this time into a deeply sarcastic smile that could have cut glass. "Of course. Why wouldn't it be? I love Vegas. It reminds me of home."

The aide looked confused, his brow furrowing as he tried to recall his geography lessons. "Slovenia?" "No," Melania replied curtly, her voice dripping with a weariness that seemed to go beyond mere jet lag. "I meant the gilded cage I call home. Now, if you'll excuse me, I have a date with a poolside cabana and the strongest cocktail this godforsaken city can muster."

As the motorcade pulled away from the airport, Trump's voice could be heard over the purr of the engines, his words floating back to the assembled press corps like verbal confetti. "You know, they named a burger after me once. The Trump Tower. 'Uge burger. Nobody could finish it. Except me, of course. I finished it in record time.

Pouli Vox

Some said it was impossible, but I did it. And that's what makes America great..."

Along with the limo motorcade, his voice and claims disappeared into the shimmering heat of the Las Vegas strip, leaving behind a wake of bewildered onlookers and the faint scent of hubris and hairspray. The reporters exchanged glances, a mixture of amusement and resignation on their faces. Another day, another spectacle.

1

THE ROMANCE

The Wynn's pool area was a clear, tranquil, and exorbitantly expensive oasis, a much-needed reprieve from the slot machines, drunken tourists, and stroke-inducing lighting that filled the rest of Las Vegas. Palm trees swayed like bored supermodels, their fronds barely stirring in the oppressive heat. Below, the water was as blue as a corporate logo, and just as shallow, reflecting the cloudless sky and the occasional private jet streaking overhead. The sleek and wealthy lounged quietly on designer chaises, their skin glistening with sunscreen that cost more per ounce than most people's monthly rent. Cabana boys in crisp, short uniforms delivered $30 cocktails with the practiced efficiency of those accustomed to catering to the whims of the ultra-rich.

In the midst of this chlorinated paradise, Melania Trump reclined in a private cabana. She had insisted on staying at the Wynn; Trump Tower's service was subpar, and she couldn't stand the thinly veiled contempt from the staff there. Now, the sun cast a warm glow over her impeccably styled caramel hair and evenly tanned legs as she leaned back. Today, she was wearing an olive swimsuit with brass buttons, and it hugged her figure like a second skin. Secretly, she loved the brass buttons on this swimsuit; they made her feel powerful, like Castro or Mussolini... iconic dictators, respected dictators. The brass buttons shone like medals, her insignia of rank. Never mind that they were purely decorative, sewn onto her swimsuit by some underpaid factory worker in a country she'd never visit. They gleamed

under
the sun, catching the light just right, and when she walked by, they might as well have been saluted by those in her vicinity.

The thought amused her, this image of herself as some kind of fashion-forward generalissimo, leading an army of sun-kissed sycophants.

WRONG

Ordering around pool staff (and the White House staff if all went well) with all the tyrannical authority of a five-star general made her smirk.

Melania Trump was no stranger to power. As she indulged in a rare moment of self-reflection, and she adjusted herself against the cushions an even rarer moment of self-appreciation. She was, after all, the neck that turned the head of the potential leader of the free world. From a small town in Slovenia to being on the road to conquering the halls of the White House like a particularly stylish Alexander the Great, she had made her way in life by playing the smart game. She had cast her lot; she had gone against every conceivable human instinct to marry something that could only loosely be characterized as a man. But this sacrifice had, in turn, granted her every taste of power and privilege she could have ever imagined. It was a heady feeling, this power. And yet...

"Still not enough power to get that buffoon out to the pool," she muttered to herself, her accent thickening with irritation.

Pouli Vox

Another excuse—this time, something about forgetting to pack his swim trunks? A lazy, ridiculous, and expected excuse as if he ever packed anything for himself in his life. In fact, she was pretty certain he had specifically ordered the staff not to pack them, probably afraid his overly-expensive spray tan would wash off in the chlorine. This was not the first time either; her dead husband had a habit of avoiding her company in private, a fact that Melania was eternally grateful for.

Her musings were interrupted by movement at the edge of her vision. She found herself looking at a strikingly attractive figure emerging poolside, flanked by an attentive, unfeasibly tall assistant handing them a towel. For once, Melania was intrigued; the figure moved with a grace that seemed almost unfair, like they had figured out some secret to life the rest of the commoners hadn't quite grasped. This was not some sunburned hedge fund manager on a bender, no; this was a creature who seemed to have sauntered out of a myth, or at least a high-end fashion magazine.

WRONG

Melania lowered her sunglasses and squinted against the harsh Nevada sun, her eyes struggling to make out details. The glare off the pool's surface created a shimmering halo around the figure, obscuring their features. Their body was lean and toned, but not overtly muscular, defying easy categorization. The way they moved was distinctive

fluid and balanced, lacking the swagger of masculinity or the sway of femininity.

She couldn't quite tell if they were... well, whatever gender they were, but she could feel an energy in them, one that was both powerful and sensual. Their golden skin gleamed in the Nevada sun, beads of water dripping down a sharp jaw. The figure's body language was refreshingly neutral, free from the exaggerated postures Melania was accustomed to seeing in the political circles she now inhabited. As she

watched, the enigmatic person accepted the towel with a graceful nod, their gestures neither masculine nor feminine, but simply... elegant. Melania found herself captivated by the aura of confidence and mystery that seemed to emanate from this captivating soul.

Pouli Vox

A flutter of attraction stirred within her, surprising in its intensity. Melania realized, with a sense of liberation, that the person's gender truly didn't matter to her. It was their presence, their energy, their ineffable quality that drew her in. In this moment, far from the scrutiny of the public eye and her husband's domineering personality, she allowed herself to acknowledge a truth she'd long suppressed: her attraction transcended the boundaries of gender.

For a moment, Melania forgot about the suffocating heat, her husband's latest antics, and the never-ending circus of the campaign. She was simply mesmerized by this person who seemed to exist beyond the rigid confines of gender, a refreshing enigma in a world of stark divisions. And in that fleeting instant, she felt a spark of something she hadn't experienced in years – genuine, unrestrained desire.

"Your Negroni Sbagliato, Sam," the assistant said, handing over a fizzing cocktail. Sam took the drink disinterestedly, their eyes fixed on Melania as a slight, appreciative smile tugged at their lips.

WRONG

Meanwhile, back behind the shield of her glasses, Melania found herself staring right back, her gaze tracing up their lithe physique. Her attention lingered on Sam's hand as it grasped the glass, watching the condensation bead and run down those long, elegant fingers. Despite herself, she found herself fantasizing: those cool, damp fingers tracing her collarbone, her spine, her... was she... was she having a bisexual fantasy!?

Well... there might just be a first time for everything, and this everything felt complex and thrilling.

Sam was having quite similar thoughts, which were written quite clearly on their face. Mrs. Trump, with her gleaming buttons and haughty expression, was the sole subject of their interest right now, which was generally a rather flighty thing. Sam was many things, after all, and refused to be defined by any of them; entrepreneur, surfer, chef, broker... the only thing that defined Sam was Sam themselves. Now, looking up the soft, ridiculously long curve of Melania's leg, Sam was damn near besotted.

Pouli Vox

"Focus, Sam," the assistant hissed, towering over Sam even though he was squatting. He was black, gay, and somewhat older than Sam; the two had known each other for years at this point. "We're here on business, remember?"

Yet Sam's eyes never left Melania. "Ah, but business and pleasure aren't mutually exclusive, my dear Max. Mrs. Trump is a unicorn—rare, beautiful, and not to be caged."

Max rolled his eyes. "She's married to Donald Trump. How rare and beautiful can she be?"

"You lack vision," Sam replied, taking a slow, cool draught of their drink. "The rather ravishing lady before you is a master strategist; after all, she's maneuvered her way to the precipice of ultimate power. I admire that in her... among other things." Smiling slightly, Sam raised their glass at

Max in a

toast, their head slightly inclined. Something in their eyes caught Melania's attention—a sort of appreciation, even respect.

Melania pretended not to notice the gesture, but she was hooked. This was different from the

WRONG

usual leering gazes she endured at hotels; Sam's interest felt... different. Carnal, yes, but she could feel more, a spark she didn't remember ever feeling before—especially not for her manchild of a husband. The figure before her was tanned, lithe, even beautiful; meanwhile, pale, white, and lumpy, Trump resembled an uncooked bratwurst whose idea of romance was a grunt and a thumbs-up. The man had all the charm of a tax audit and the sensitivity of a bulldozer, yet there he was, sprawled across her life like a bloated manatee.

Occasionally, she'd catch a glimpse of him waddling around their opulent home in his bathrobe, looking like a bedraggled emperor who had misplaced his empire. And she'd wonder, not for the first time, how she ended up here, playing the role of the dutiful wife in this absurd, reality-TV version of a marriage.

"I want to send her a gift," Sam declared, sitting up at the side of the pool, water dripping down their hair. "Something from... let's say Cartier, the Panthère de Cartier collection. After all, nothing says 'I see you' like giving her a panther- wild,

Pouli Vox

fearless, dangerous- I know a cunning animal when I see it."

Max sighed. "And I know trouble when I see it. Nothing says lawsuit quite like pursuing the potential First Lady."

As Sam and the assistant appeared to be approached ~~bickering~~ ~~a pool~~ ~~Melanias cabana, all smiles and attendant~~ muscles. The wind whipped his dirty blonde hair as he leaned over, flexing his biceps in the least subtle gesture Melania had ever seen.

"Can I get you anything, Mrs. Trump? Perhaps some... lotion?" he asked in a semi-pleasant drawl, staring at Melania with a deep, meaningful gaze.

Melania fixed him with an icy stare. The spell, so fleeting, was now broken. "Yes. I need someone to rub sunscreen on my back. Fetch my husband, would you?"

The color drained from the pool attendant's face as his bravado took a quick dive. "I... uh... of

WRONG

course, Mrs. Trump. Right away." He scurried off, leaving Melania to her thoughts.

She found her gaze and thoughts drifting back to Sam, though this time her fantasies were less saucy and more... well, girlish. On another day she would have scoffed at herself, but she found herself wondering... what would it be like to be cherished, adored? To have someone appreciate the cunning beneath her beauty? The possibility of a connection—intellectual, emotional, and yes, perhaps even physical—with someone so intriguing sent a thrill through her.

Now, Melania's thoughts oscillated between taking stock of her current portfolio and the tantalizing freedom a path with Sam represented. She was the neck that turned the head, yes—but perhaps it was time for that neck to consider a different direction entirely. As she contemplated this, a startling clarity washed over her. With or without Sam, she knew deep in her bones that she would be better off without Trump. The realization wasn't new, but its intensity was.

Years of suppressing her own desires, of playing the dutiful wife to a man whose ego consumed everything in its path, had taken their toll. She'd known it for a long time, but now, standing here in the sweltering Las Vegas heat, watching Sam's lithe form disappear into the crowd, the truth felt more urgent than ever.

Trump was an anchor, dragging her down into depths she no longer wanted to explore. Whether her future included Sam or not, Melania suddenly understood with crystal clarity that her course forward—her path to genuine happiness and fulfillment—lay decisively away from the man she had married.

2

THE ROMAN EMPIRE

When a stupid man is doing something, he is ashamed of, he always declares that it is his duty.

George Bernard Shaw once said that—and it's a quote that's been trotted out by armchair philosophers and pretentious college students alike. Of course, Shaw wasn't thinking about Donald Trump when he said it, who had long outlived anything resembling shame in his dusty little heart. Even as his wife was enjoying herself a little too much at the pool, the Trump in question was pacing his lavish suite at the Wynn, patently oblivious to anything beyond his own inflated sense of self-importance.

The suite, a monument to excess and questionable taste, gleamed with enough gold to make Midas himself blush. Trump paused

Pouli Vox

occasionally to admire his reflection in the gold-trimmed mirrors that seemed to occupy every available wall space. He looked good—no, great. The idea of joining Melania at the pool had crossed his mind for about two seconds before he quickly dismissed it. His complexion, carefully cultivated through years of tanning beds and spray-on solutions, was far too precious to risk in the harsh Nevada sun.

"As if," he muttered to himself, his voice echoing in the cavernous room. "Those paparazzi vultures would love to get a shot of me." He snorted, imagining the headlines. They'd say he was 240, maybe 241—fake news. They'd probably doctor the photos too, make him look bloated.

"Then they'd start yapping about how I'm not

the

perfect 239 pounds I've told them. Wrong!"

He gave the mirror a defiant look, as if daring it to disagree. But of course, the mirror was on his side, reflecting back exactly what he wanted to see: a strong, powerful man in his prime.

Luscious golden locks fluttered in the AC with all the resplendence of a moth caught inside a coffin; pouting lips drooped in an eternal frown.

WRONG

Now this was a man's man—the kind of man who didn't have time for swimming pools or sunbathing, not when there were important deals to be made. After all, he was a business genius, the likes of which the world had never seen. He had the Midas touch, turning everything he laid his small, sausage-like fingers on into pure gold. Well, maybe not pure gold, but at least chipped golden paint that could fool the voters for a while.

Now, pausing at the side of his great, remarkably uncluttered desk, he glanced at the stack of note cards arranged squarely in the middle. The stark white of the cards contrasted sharply with the deep mahogany of the desk, like islands of potential knowledge in a sea of polished ignorance.

The human brain is capable of generating a staggering number of ideas per minute; in fact, the human mind's creativity and desire to be stimulated is what led to mankind shanking all its competition into the ground with sharp sticks. From there on, mankind was busy settling river valleys, making sculptures, and discovering new and strange places— however, none of this evolutionary wit and creativity had made it over to

Pouli Vox

this specimen of Homo Trumpus. Because of this, his team had decided that he dearly needed these tastelessly embossed cards for tonight's fundraiser, for each was filled with talking points and dubious statistics. A lot of work had gone into preparing those cards—thankfully, none of it had been his.

He didn't read them, though. His advisors had been begging him to, but to expect work from him was simply wrong. He was, after all, not a worker; he was a winner, and winners wing it. Trump chuckled patronizingly as he looked at the cards; why read these? He already knew exactly how to misread a room, and always had a lot to talk about, even if he hadn't the faintest idea about anything at all. Why spend hours memorizing talking points when you could just walk in, flash that million-dollar smile, and let that good, old-fashioned charm do the rest?

He picked up one of the cards, skimmed it for about 2.13 seconds, then tossed it aside with the casual disregard of a man who believed facts were merely suggestions.

Boring.

WRONG

Who wrote this stuff anyway? Probably one of those pencil-pushers in Washington who had never made a real deal in their life. Tonight, he'd go in, say a few words, make a few incredible jokes... and then let the donations roll in.

Simple. Just then, Donald's stomach grumbled, the

sound echoing in the vast suite like a distant thunderclap. Closing his eyes sagely, he knew what time it was: second breakfast, the most important meal of the day. Well, they were all important, but this one held a special place in his heart, somewhere between First Breakfast, and Early Lunch Because I'm Important, damn It.

Feeling another grumble, he reached for the phone on his desk, his fingers dancing across the keypad with the grace of a drunken elephant attempting ballet.

He'd recently heard (someone mentioned it on Fox) that Roman emperors ate figs to increase their virility, and to become leaner men, real men. Not that he needed any help in that department.

Pouli Vox

He was certain he had the best stamina, the best energy, maybe in the history of presidential candidates—so much so that his wife hadn't slept with him in months, afraid of his sexual prowess. The thought made him puff out his chest, blissfully unaware of the true reasons behind Melania's distance.

But figs were a sign of royalty, and if anyone in America was practically royalty, it was him. He was the closest thing the country had to a king, really. Well, maybe more of an emperor.

Yeah, that sounded better. He grabbed the

phone, his voice booming with
the authority of a man used to getting his way. "Hello, this is Donald Trump. I need figs. The best figs. And in a gold bowl. Your most golden bowl."
"Uh, pardon me, sir," came a nasal voice, tinged with confusion. "Did you say... pigs?"
"No, you shit-whistle! Figs! F-I-G-S! Little fruit things! Like raisins but not shriveled up and, and... sad. I want the biggest, juiciest figs you've ever seen! The juiciest figs ever seen, in fact."

WRONG

The voice on the other end paused, clearly struggling to process the request. "I'm afraid... we, uh... don't have those on our menu, Mr. Trump. We have apples, bananas—"

"Apples? Bananas? What am I, a monkey? I said figs! Figs are classy. Everyone loves figs! The Romans loved them. Great people, the Romans... but that's not the point. Figs. Get me some!"
"Uh, we could offer a fruit platter, sir." "Any figs in

it?" "...I'm afraid not." "Are you kidding me? What

kind of second-rate
operation are you running? I could get figs on Air Force One, and that was a government plane!

You
can't even manage a simple bowl of figs? What, did you run out?"

"Um, we actually never have them, sir." Trump's

face contorted into a mask of
indignation, his cheeks flushing a shade of red

Pouli Vox

that clashed horribly with his artificial tan. "Get me those figs, or I'll make sure you're serving hot dogs on the street corner by the end of the week!" he whined, his voice rising to a pitch that threatened to shatter the crystal chandeliers.

"Sir, I'm sorry, but we can't—"

"Can't? Can't? What is it with people and 'can't'? I never say 'can't.' That's why I'm Donald Trump."
"Again, I'm sorry sir, but—"

Trump slammed down the phone with enough force to make the desk rattle. "Useless! Absolutely useless! Don't they know who I am? I'm practically the President- I'm going to be the President, and then they'll see!"

Grumbling, Trump made his way to the elevator, his gait a curious mixture of a waddle and a strut. As he trudged through the corridors like a disgruntled toad, he muttered to himself, "If there was a Wynn in Rome, they would've had..." his thoughts trailing before finished... "they never had to put up with folks like this, the worst."

WRONG

Back in the good ol' days, of course, the Romans could kill servants who didn't obey their betters. Look how subpar service was now. He should be served as an emperor, surrounded by adoring subjects, perhaps with a ceremonial guard, some sort of golden laurel wreath, and definitely someone fanning him with palm fronds—preferably an attractive assistant who wouldn't make eye contact and was trained not to ask too many questions.

Instead, the elevator doors dinged open with all the drama of a washing machine cycle, and he was greeted by the sight of a bellhop. If one cared to know, one would find out that he was a hobbyist guitarist. In fact, if he had ever been fired, the bellhop would undoubtedly have become one of the greatest guitarists in the world—unfortunately, he was simply too good at being ordered around.

"Going down?" the bellhop asked cheerfully, his smile so wide it threatened to split his face in two.
"Yeah, down. Down to the lobby. So, What."
Trump grunted, stepping into the elevator with all the grace of a rhinoceros attempting ballet.

Pouli Vox

"Of course, sir. Right away."

As they reached the lobby, Trump stormed out of the elevator, his presence parting the crowd like a tangerine-tinted Moses. At this point, it should

be stated that the Wynn's lobby was, like much of Vegas, allergic to normalcy; someone in the design phase had clearly decided that too much was just the right amount, because the first impression one got of the Wynn was a fairytale gone wrong. The ceiling soared, the chandeliers dripped, and the floor looked like someone's acid trip. In the midst of this mess, the plant life had seemingly mutated into a botanical zoo, covered in lights, sequins, and what certainly looked like someone's underwear.

Of course, our intrepid protagonist cared nothing about this—he was a man of sheer, misplaced focus. As Trump charged through the forested lobby like a mildly deranged knight, a confused hostess tried to stop him.

"Excuse me, sir, you can't—"

WRONG

"Out of my way! I'm going in there! No figs, they tell me. What sort of place keeps no figs?!"

The Wynn's ever-observant manager, catching wind of the commotion, rushed over, his face a mask of professional concern. "Mr. Trump, what seems to be the issue?"

"What's the issue? The issue is I'm hungry! I know it may be an exception request, but you're exceptional people, aren't you? I want figs. Figs! The best figs, not the cheap stuff. Imperial quality figs, and they're going to be good. I'm going to make sure they're good, sweet, juicy... So, I'm going in the kitchen."

"Sir, I'm afraid I can't let you..." the manager paused, his mind racing to find a diplomatic way to deny the request. "Sir, I'm not sure room service figs are a thing..."

"Do you know who I am?" Trump scowled mid-tantrum, his face contorting into an expression that would make a bulldog look photogenic. "I helped build this place, ask anyone. I helped... it wouldn't exist without me, that's what I'm saying.

Pouli Vox

That's right. Now, you're going to stop me from going into the kitchen? Unbelievable. You're lucky to even have a job!"

The professional manager blanched, his
demeanor cracking under the weight of Trump's tirade. "Mr. Trump, please, I'll get the figs for you. Just, please, stay here in the lobby."
"Fine, fine. But they better be the best figs. And remember, I want them in a golden bowl. The best. If it's not gold, it's garbage."

The manager nodded frantically and sprinted off, leaving behind a faint trail of flop sweat and desperation. Trump watched him go, scowling after him impatiently. Fifteen minutes later, the manager returned, sweating and out of breath, holding a plate of figs that looked like they had decorative
been hastily plucked from a arrangement.
"Here you are, Mr. Trump. Fresh figs." Trump

glanced at the plate, then scowled.
"Where's the golden bowl? I said golden bowl! Do you not listen? Unbelievable. This is why this

WRONG

place isn't what it used to be. The service is going downhill. I want gold. Do you think that Caesar guy ate on a plate? Gold!"

"Mr. Trump, I'm sorry, we didn't have..."

"Save it. I'll be having words later." Trump shot him a pointed look before storming back towards the elevator, the plate of figs clutched in his hand like a conquered territory. Again, the bellboy greeted him with a docile smile that seemed permanently etched onto his face.
"Up, sir?"

Trump grunted. He had a fig in his mouth.

The elevator dinged on the first floor as a young boy stepped in. He was perhaps ten years old, scrolling through a smartphone with the practiced indifference of youth.
Perfect, Trump thought: a prime candidate to test his ability to work the room. As if he needed the help of some shitty, underpaid writer to give him talking points. He'd show them all how a real leader connects with the common folk.

Pouli Vox

Trump smiled at the kid with his beady little eyes, a gesture that made him look generally constipated. "Hey, kid. You know who I am?"

"Uh-huh," the boy responded without looking up, his tone suggesting he'd rather be anywhere else. Silence. Trump popped another fig into his mouth, chewing thoughtfully.
"I once arm-wrestled Putin, you know. Beat him so bad, he cried. True story," he chuckled, puffing out his chest with pride.

The kid nodded, bored. Trump's smirk faltered, but he pressed on, determined to impress.
"Yeah, Putin. You know, right? This big. Big guy, tough guy. Russian. But I beat him. Nobody talks about it, because of woke. Media stuff, you're, you're too young for that. But I did it— tremendous
win. You should've seen it." The kid looked up, his

face a mask of
unimpressed pre-teen cynicism. "Mister, you

WRONG

need to chew your food better. And dad says you shouldn't talk with your mouth full. It's rude."

Trump nearly choked on his fig, his face turning a shade of purple that clashed horribly with his orange hue.

"You know what your dad is, kid? Wrong!" he barked as the elevator dinged to a stop. He turned to the bellhop, his voice rising to a pitch that threatened to shatter the mirrors lining the elevator. "You! Yeah, you! When you're done babysitting, I need you to fetch me more figs, I'm already almost through all of these"

The bellhop nodded eagerly, his smile never wavering. "Of course, Mr. Trump! Right away!" As Trump waddled off, muttering something under his breath about ungrateful youth and the decline of American values, the bellhop turned to the boy. "Can you believe that? Donald Trump just gave me an order!"

The boy sighed, shaking his head with the world-weariness of someone three times his age. "Yeah, and if you're smart, you'll ignore it."

Pouli Vox

Big Don shuffled back to his room, slamming the door behind him with enough force to make the gaudy artwork on the walls rattle. He tossed a slightly dry piece of fruit into his mouth, chewing without enthusiasm. The remaining fruit landed unceremoniously in a bowl on the end table. He barely spared them a glance as he set them down, suggesting he'd had more than his fill of nature's bounty and now in fact, our protagonist had moved onto bigger things—like an issue of Playboy he'd been hiding from his wife for months.

The bowl of figs sat on the table, the faux-gold paint glinting in the room's warm lights. It was a symbol of power, decadence, and an empire in the making. Trump settled into an overstuffed armchair, magazine in hand, blissfully unaware of the ironies surrounding him.
Of course, there's a little problem with empires.

They tend to fall.

3

CONSPIRACY

The Heart Attack Café buzzed with nervous energy, a hive of anticipation and trepidation. Republicans were about to roll in like a red tide, and the staff was in a frenzy, scurrying about like ants whose hill had just been kicked. Amidst the chaos, Nico, the unofficial kitchen leader, stood as an island of calm. With his floppy hair, warm smile, and steady hands, Nico had earned the respect of the entire staff through his unflappable demeanor and culinary prowess. He surveyed the kitchen, chuckling to himself as he watched his coworkers scurry about like caffeinated squirrels, pots clanging and orders being shouted across the steamy space.
The Heart Attack Café was, in a word... garish. Red dominated what passed for décor—red

booths, red walls, even the ceiling was a heinous shade of red that seemed to pulse with each beat of the rock music blaring from hidden speakers. The atmosphere was a bizarre blend of hospital and greasy spoon diner, as waitresses dressed as casting-couch nurses moved through the ogling diners, serving up massive burgers that could rival the size of a small car. The air was thick with the sound of arteries clogging, and coronaries in real-time.

Unbeknownst to the kitchen staff, Vic Greene, the Heart Attack Café Manager, lurked just outside the door, eavesdropping with the intensity of a spy on a crucial mission. Vic was a scrawny man with nervous energy and a scraggly goatee, his uniform hanging loosely on his bony frame like a sail on a mast. He ran a hand through his thinning hair, his mind always racing with possibilities, each more outlandish than the last.

Vic had always resented Nico's easy popularity, the way the staff gravitated towards him despite the manager's higher position. And those waitresses, with their skimpy "nurse" outfits, getting all the attention while he was ignored. It wasn't fair. He was an American Patriot, damn it!

WRONG

He deserved his spot as Manager and he deserved his shot at fame and fortune. His fingers twitched at his sides, itching to grasp the success that always seemed just out of reach.

As he listened to the staff's joking plots about adding "special ingredients" to Trump's meal, an idea began to form in Vic's mind, unfurling like a poisonous flower. If something were to happen to Trump on his watch, he'd be famous. Maybe even get his own reality show. "Heart Attack Café: High Stakes Dining." Though he preferred Trump to win over anyone else running, the 15 minutes of fame- no, the lifetime of fame that would come from being the one that took out Donald Trump would make more difference to his life than anything that Trump might actually accomplish as a politician. The thought made his heart race with excitement, a giddy rush of adrenaline coursing through his veins.

He pushed through the kitchen doors, his entrance silencing the staff mid-joke. The sudden quiet was as if someone had hit a mute button on the chaos.

Pouli Vox

"Listen up, you miscreants," he announced, trying to puff out his chest but only succeeding in making his collar bones more pronounced. "I couldn't help but overhear your little... brainstorming session."

Nico stepped forward, his calm demeanor a stark contrast to Vic's manic energy. He was ready to defend his team, but Vic held up a pale hand, his dirty fingernails now on display.
"Now, now, Nico. No need to be a hero. In fact, I think you guys might be onto something."
The kitchen fell silent, confusion evident on every face. The only sound was the sizzle of burgers on the grill and the distant chatter of diners. "Boss?"

Nico ventured cautiously; his voice laced with concern. "What are you saying?"
Vic's eyes gleamed with a mix of desperation and ambition, like a man on the edge of a cliff contemplating the view. "I'm saying, if you folks really want to make a statement tonight, I might be willing to... look the other way."

WRONG

Nico's eyes widened in disbelief, his usually unflappable demeanor cracking. "You can't be serious. We were joking!"

"Were you?" Vic challenged, scanning the uncertain faces around him. His gaze was intense, almost feverish. "Because I'm not. Think about it. One little 'accident,' and we could change the course of history. Make America great again... for real this time."

The silence in the kitchen was deafening, broken only by the hiss of the grill and the distant chatter of diners. Nico looked around at his coworkers, seeing a mix of temptation and fear in their eyes. He took a deep breath, knowing he had to be the voice of reason in this sea of madness.

"No," Nico said firmly, his eyes locked on Vic's. His voice was steady, a counterpoint to Vic's manic energy. "That's not us. The crew jokes around during prep, but when it comes down to it, we're just here to work—to serve good food. We're not getting mixed up in any political agenda nonsense. Listen, we don't want trouble. Getting involved would only make things worse for us, not better. Think about it: if we actually did something like that, we'd be playing right into their hands. They already think anyone who speaks Spanish and works in a kitchen is some kind of criminal. We understand the stakes better than you might realize. It's not worth confirming their prejudices."

Vic's face darkened, his ambition turning to anger. The change was palpable, like a storm rolling in. "You're making a mistake, Nico. This could be our chance—my chance—to really make a difference. To be somebody!"

Nico stood his ground; his calm resolves a stark contrast to Vic's increasing agitation. "We make a difference every day, Vic, for our lives and our families by showing up with pride and integrity. That's the America we believe in, Vic." Nico said, looking slightly annoyed at having to explain the morality in living an honest, good life.

For a moment, it seemed like Vic might explode, his face turning a shade of red that rivaled the café's décor. But then he deflated, the madness fading from his eyes, replaced by a cold determination. "Fine," he grumbled, his voice low and dangerous. "But don't come crying to me

WRONG

when your precious integrity doesn't pay the bills. Or when you're deported," he added under his breath, the words barely audible but dripping with venom.

As Vic stormed out, the kitchen collectively exhaled, the tension dissipating like steam from a kettle. Nico turned to his team, a small smile on his face, trying to restore normalcy. "Alright, let's get back to work. We've got some heart attacks to
serve... the old-fashioned way," he said, a charming smile on his face.

The staff chuckled nervously, the tension slowly dissipating. As they returned to their stations, the familiar rhythm of the kitchen slowly returning, Nico couldn't help but wonder what the night would bring. One thing was certain: it was going to be a dinner service to remember.

Meanwhile, Vic retreated to his shared office desk, his mind racing faster than a hamster on a wheel. If Nico and his goody-two-shoes crew with
morals wouldn't help, he'd have to take matters into his own hands. After all, wasn't that the true American way? Taking initiative, seizing

41

opportunity? The thought made him feel powerful, important.

He glanced at the nameplate on his desk. "Victor" it read in bold, generic font. He grimaced, remembering how he always told people his name was short for "Victory" but no one ever remembered, or perhaps thought he was joking. But it was one of the few things he was genuinely proud of. "My parents knew I was destined for greatness," he'd boast to anyone who'd listen. "They named me Victory for a reason."

Vic's eyes then moved to the framed photo next to the nameplate—a younger Vic, smiling hopefully in front of the Hollywood sign. The photo was slightly faded, the edges curling, but the hope in young Vic's eyes was still clearly visible. It was a stark contrast to the bitter, desperate man he'd become.

"This is my shot," he whispered to himself, a manic gleam in his eye. His reflection in the computer screen showed a man on the edge, teetering between desperation and delusion. "My one chance at the big time. And I'm not going to

WRONG

let anyone stand in my way. After all, I'm Victory. It's in my name, for crying out loud!"

With trembling hands, Vic began to plot. The Heart Attack Café was about to live up to its name in ways no one could have anticipated. And Vic "Victory" Greene was determined to be at the center of it all, finally living up to the grand destiny his name promised. As he scribbled furiously on a notepad, his handwriting barely legible in his excitement, Vic failed to notice the irony of his situation. In his quest for fame and recognition, he was about to cook up a scheme that could very well be his own undoing.

The kitchen continued its chaotic dance of preparation, unaware of the storm brewing in Vic's mind. As the hour of Trump's arrival drew nearer, the air in the Heart Attack Café grew thicker with anticipation, grease, and the unmistakable scent of impending disaster.

4

PREPPING

They say it takes a hero to preach the truth. In fact, it takes an even bigger hero with an ego to preach something that is nowhere close to truth.

After all, the sheer strength of will, intelligence, and perseverance needed to go against all the odds for the sake of something utterly and incredibly stupid is a feat in itself. This feat was performed one – that Donald Trump had consistently throughout his life, being the hero no one had asked for and no one deserved.

Yet he had persevered nonetheless, like a particularly stubborn weed growing through cracks in the sidewalk of reality.

WRONG

At this moment, our utterly unneeded messiah was lounging on a plush sofa in his private suite at the Wynn. The sofa was a monstrosity of gold leaf and piss-yellow brocade that had been requested especially for his visits. Any sane individual, upon seeing this affront to furniture, would have immediately reached for the matches, but Mr. Trump adored it. After all, it was big, loud, and obnoxious, and so fit the Trumpian aesthetic completely. It cradled his ample form like a gaudy throne, a fitting seat for a man who saw himself as American royalty.

Trump's prodigious mind, such as it was, was focused on a far more pressing matter than his in interior design, or the weight of concentration, creating new valleys in the orange responsibilities. His landscape of his face. brow furrowed Prepping.

Everyone kept yammering about "prepping" for tonight's fundraiser at the Heart Attack Café. As if he needed to prep for anything. Trump scoffed, his lips curling in a way that was only loosely human, more reminiscent of a fish gasping for air than a presidential candidate contemplating his strategy. Prepping was for losers and people who weren't him. The word itself seemed to carry a feeling of weakness, something you'd find lingering around a failed Democratic candidate or maybe a contestant who'd choked during the third round of The Apprentice.

He was Donald Trump, for crying out loud. The name itself, he believed, was a preparation for greatness. "I'm Donald Trump," he repeated to

the empty
room, his voice bouncing off the skeptical walls like a poorly thought-out declaration of war. The words hung in the air, as if even they were embarrassed to be associated with him. "I don't prep. I win." He turned to a mirror, giving it a grin he thought was particularly dazzling. It most closely resembled a wrinkled shrimp attempting to sell used cars. His eyes reluctantly drifted

toward the stack of
briefing papers on the nearby desk, which had multiplied exponentially since he last glanced at them; by now, the stack was thick enough to smash a small mouse into a pancake. The

WRONG

additional papers had been dropped off by some frazzled aide who looked like he'd never eaten a cheeseburger in his life—practically a walking skeleton with a bad haircut and worse suit.

Unwillingly, he flipped open the top folder, giving it the kind of half-hearted attention he usually reserved for celebrity endorsements that didn't include his name. Someone had typed up a memo about tonight's guest list, full of names that sounded like brands of knockoff Italian wine. He could never keep track of these people—donors, lobbyists, other, lesser politicians... They all blurred together in his mind, a sea of faceless sycophants whose only purpose was to bask in his greatness.

The only name that stood out to him was his favorite: TRUMP. He liked seeing it in print, especially when it was bolded. It was like a beacon of self-importance, shining through the significant

dreary landscape of other, less names.
But even that lost its charm after a few seconds. He slammed the folder shut with a satisfying thwack, satisfied that he'd done his due

diligence. Whatever happened at the campaign stop, he'd wing it. He always did, and it always ~~work~~ed out. His best moments spontaneous, like when he'd thrown those paper towels in Puerto Rico. Nobody had ever seen anything like it. People loved it. Even the fake news couldn't deny the genius in it. At least, that's what he told himself as he basked in the glow of his own perceived brilliance.

Just then, the big black hotel phone on the desk buzzed, the sound cutting through his self-congratulatory reverie like a knife through butter. Trump ignored it at first, but the buzzing continued, more insistent now, like the time Rudy had tried to convince him that his hair dye was waterproof. Reluctantly, Trump picked up the rather girthy receiver, with the thought of reprimanding whoever was on the other end for interrupting his important task of admiring himself.

"Yeah?" he barked into the phone, his voice a mixture of annoyance and barely concealed ignorance.

WRONG

"Mr. Trump, it's about tonight's fundraiser. Ahem, we just wanted to go over the talking points again..." The voice on the other end was tentative, clearly bracing for the storm that was about to hit.

"Talking points? Shit-sticks. I don't need talking points. I'm Trump. My whole life is a talking point, of thousands of people know this, right?" His voice ask anyone. Thousands of thousands rose in volume and pitch, threatening to shatter the crystal chandeliers.

"Y...yes sir, but..." The poor aide on the other end sounded like he was considering a career change, perhaps to something less stressful, like defusing bombs.

"Right. So, I know what I'm doing. I know. I'll tell you what to do, listen." Trump's voice took on the tone of a man explaining rocket science to a particularly dim-witted child.

"Oh. Sir, I don't think you need to..."

"You look them in the eye, like this, and you tell them about the wall, the economy, whatever. Make a funny joke about some bums. They'll love it, alright. Trust me. That's a Trump guarantee, the best kind of guarantee."

Trump hung up with enough force to make the desk rattle, frowning petulantly. He couldn't get over how everyone always thought they knew better than him. It was one of the great mysteries of life, like how windmills caused cancer or why food tasted better when it had at least a 20% chance of causing heart disease. Briefly, he

wondered where Melania was, not that it mattered much. She had insisted on separate suites this time, something about needing her own space or wanting to enjoy her "welcome basket" in peace. Trump didn't see the appeal. A welcome basket was usually some nuts, dried fruit, maybe a little brie if the place was fancy. He liked brie, but it wasn't worth a separate suite. The concept of personal space was as foreign to him as empathy or fiscal responsibility.

Trump snorted to himself, a sound not unlike a

pig
rooting for truffles. He knew she was probably down at the spa, getting pampered or whatever it was women did when they weren't admiring him. He'd never understood the appeal of spa

WRONG

treatments, all those oils and stones and whatnot. If he wanted to relax, he'd just watch recordings of his best interviews, basking in the glow of his own perceived brilliance.

But all in all, Trump was secretly glad for the private suite. After all, you never know when you might want the privacy... a man never knew where the night might lead in Las Vegas. Maybe he'd order up one of those personal massages he'd heard so much about, something as decadent and morally bankrupt as possible, like that wonderful, pungent night in Moscow....

As his mind wandered down paths best left unexplored, he suddenly remembered a joke someone had made about his "mis-sized pickles" once. He'd never understood why that was funny. Pickles came in all sizes, didn't they? And his were the best sizes, tremendous sizes. He made a mental note to ask his PA about it later, though he'd likely forget before the thought fully formed. But before he could entertain those possibilities further, a low, ominous gurgle emanated from his midsection. He paused, his soulless little eyes squinting as he tried to remember what he'd eaten, doubling over as his lips formed a tiny little 'o'.

Then, realization dawned, hitting him with all the subtlety of a freight train.

"Oo, the fig. The Roman freaking figs!" This gurgle

was followed by a sharp, insistent cramping sensation that went shooting through his abdomen like a tweet that hadn't been spell-checked. It was as if his intestines had suddenly decided to stage a revolt against their despotic ruler.

"No, no, no," Trump muttered, clutching his stomach with soft, pudgy hands that hadn't worked a day in their life. "Not now. Not now. I'm too... well, I haven't approved of this..."

But the cramps persisted, a series of waves that felt as if his very digestive tract had turned democratic. It wasn't supposed to be like this. He was a great man, an important man. And his diet was simple, foolproof: steaks, candy, and the occasional cardiac-arrest-inducing whopper. His body had never betrayed him like this before, at

WRONG

least not in a way he couldn't ignore or blame on someone else.

As he waddled towards the bathroom like a remarkably wrinkled sow in the throes of childbirth, Trump wondered at his own genius. Insisting on a private suite had been an amazing idea, a brilliant one even—because whatever our spray-tanned hero was about to witness, was definitely not fit for public consumption.

The bathroom door loomed before him, a porcelain portal to what promised to be a humbling experience. As he reached for the handle, another cramp hit him, causing him to double over. In that moment, Donald Trump, the man who would be king, was reduced to nothing more than a victim of his own excess, about to face off against the most formidable opponent of his career: his own vanity, manifested in the form of a bowel movement of biblical proportion.

5

PULLING THREADS

The neon lights of Las Vegas buzzed like a swarm of hyperactive ghosts, casting an eerie glow that seeped into the Assassin's hotel room despite his best efforts to cocoon himself from the outside world. The expensive curtains, a shade of beige that screamed "luxury accommodation," did little to block out the city's relentless luminescence. Technically, it wasn't exactly his hotel room—it belonged to a sleazy old man who was currently bound up and pissing himself somewhere in a gutter. His shiny black card, on the other hand, had afforded the Assassin an in to the Wynn, an establishment that made him wrinkle his nose with its garish vomitous displays of class.

He was sitting on that one entirely irrelevant and unneeded chair available in most hotel rooms, generally designated for swingers or people who

WRONG

enjoy brooding. Too single for the former, the Assassin was having a good old brooding session as he cleaned his piano-wire and knife set, his gloved hands working with the precision of a pianist with a gun to his head. The metallic gleam of his tools contrasted sharply with the dull, worn fabric of the chair, a visual metaphor for the disparity between his chosen profession and his current surroundings.

He was a distinguished looking man, with the salt and pepper hair reminiscent of old money, even though his bank account most resembled that of the average middle-class coffee barista. His neatly trimmed beard bristled as he snorted with the patented self-loathing of someone nearly half a century old. The lines on his face told a story of a life lived hard and fast, with more regrets than he cared to count.

At 47, he felt every one of his years, plus a few extra for good measure. **If his stocks hadn't nosedived harder than a kamikaze pilot, he wouldn't be here doing more of Jeffrey's dirty work. But life, as it turned out, had a sick sense of humor. One minute you're toasting your financial genius, the next you're scrounging for painkillers and cursing the day you learned to spell 'diversify' and have lunch with the Palm Beach elite.

He checked his watch, a cheap knockoff that always managed to be 15 minutes behind, much like his life choices. A heavy sigh escaped his lips; another day, another name to cross off Jeffrey's seemingly endless list of "loose ends" from some shadowy billionaires' club. This one last job business was getting out of hand. If he didn't know better, he'd swear Jeffrey was just making names up to keep him busy, like some sort of twisted game of assassin's bingo.
"Cunty prick," he muttered to himself, blowing into the nozzle of his somewhat-silenced Luger. The familiar weight of the gun in his hand brought a grim comfort, a reminder of simpler times when his biggest worry was whether to use a 9mm or a .45.
The Assassin had met a lot of characters in his line of work, but Jeffrey was something else entirely. Jeffrey had made it big in some convoluted business scheme involving luxury cleaning
supplies. How that led to a pan-Atlantic drug

tomatoes, semi-fresh brie, and

WRONG

empire and human trafficking operation was anyone's guess. As for the assassin business, that was just an international operation that Jeffrey ran on the side, mostly as a hobby. The whole thing sounded like a bad plot from a straight-to-DVD movie, but here he was, living it.

The Assassin stretched, wincing as his joints popped. He had no real opinion on tonight's target; the most he knew about Trump was that he was a businessman of some description, had an interest in making a wall of some sort, and had gone on more than a few questionable vacations with the Assassin's now employer. The Assassin wasn't the most politically involved man—the most politically active he got was when it came to killing Jeffrey's "loose ends", which couldn't be all that bad he figured, he liked to think of it as doing his public duty—and looking at the picture of his primordially absurd client, he suddenly had the feeling that he was about to do mankind a serious favor with this job.

"Alright, let's get this over with," he sighed to himself, adjusting his gear one last time. The familiar routine of checking his weapons and equipment brought a sense of calm, a stark contrast to the chaos of his thoughts. He had no idea how many more of these one-last-jobs he had lined up this week, and frankly, he had plenty of shows to catch up on. The irony of worrying about his Netflix queue while preparing to assassinate a presidential candidate wasn't lost on him.

The Assassin slipped out of his room and into the gaudy hallway, his movements as fluid and silent as a shadow. Trump's suite was just across the way, the oversized door screaming 'I have more money than taste'. He could practically smell the spray tan and vainglory seeping through the cracks, a pungent reminder of the excess his target embodied.

Just as he was pondering his entry strategy, a pleasant and somewhat idiotic looking bellhop rolled past him with a room service cart, coming to a stop outside Trump's door. The Assassin felt a pang of guilt for what he was about to do, though it passed quicker than a Vegas marriage. With a series of moves that made his joints protest, he somewhat quickly, somewhat clumsily subdued the bellhop and stashed him in

WRONG

his own room. The poor guy would wake up with a headache and a story no one would believe.

Donning the bellhop's jacket and hat, which fit about as well as his current life choices, the Assassin returned to the hallway and pushed the cart up to Trump's door. As he raised his fist to knock, a strange, muffled sound reached his ears. It was coming from inside the room. The Assassin frowned and leaned in against the door, pressing his ear to it; what greeted him was a collection of whimpers that sounded a bit like a humpback whale having a passionate round of self-love.

"Oh, for the love of...please don't be what I think it is," he muttered to himself, his hand hovering uncertainly before rapping on the door. "Room service," he called out, trying to sound bored rather than nauseated.

The noises from inside the room continued without pause, with the orchestra joined by the low, melodic whistle of a fart. The Assassin shut his eyes with a sense of calm, cosmic disgust as he weighed his options. On one hand, he could break in, get this over with quickly. But...getting in would mean confronting whatever ungodly scene was happening on the other side of the door. The sounds coming from within painted a picture he'd rather not see in high definition.

"I'm getting too old for this shit," he grumbled under his breath, thinking back to the days when his biggest worry was picking out the right scope. Now here he was, contemplating whether to one-man interrupt what sounded like a reenactment of the Battle of Waterloo, but with more gas.

With a pained grimace, the Assassin rammed the cart against the door one last time, hoping to every deity he'd ever come across that it would be enough to put an end to whatever was happening in there. But instead of silence, he was met with a strangled cry from inside:
"No! No, no!"

The Assassin blanched, his face turning a shade of white that would make a ghost jealous.
That was it. That was the final straw. Whatever in the actual horrors were going on in there, it

WRONG

smelled in a fantastical way that was way, way above his pay grade. This was not what he signed up for when he decided to become a hired killer. Murder? Fine. Political intrigue? Sure. But this... this was a bridge too far.

"Nope. Not today. Not ever," the Assassin declared, abandoning the cart like a rat fleeing a sinking ship. Some things were just not worth the money, and whatever was happening behind that door definitely fell into that category.

He turned on his heel and hobbled as fast as his aching joints would allow, back down the hallway toward the elevator. He'd catch up with his target later, yes, at that heart attack joint down the street he was scheduled to appear at later, at least then he'd have his pants up, most likely. But right now, he needed about a gallon of brain bleach and a stiff drink. Maybe a few stiff drinks. Hell, maybe the whole bottle.

The elevator dinged; a cheerful sound that felt wildly inappropriate given the circumstances. The Assassin stepped in, sighing as he leaned against the mirrored wall. His reflection stared back at him, a middle-aged man in an ill-fitting

Pouli Vox

bellhop uniform, questioning every life choice that had led him to this moment.

"I wonder if I can afford therapy after this job," he mused as the doors folded shut like metal curtains, leaving behind the sounds of whatever ungodly scene was unfolding in Trump's suite. He'd have to find another way to deliver Jeffrey's message: "Jeffrey's tying up loose ends, your time has come." But that could wait. For now, he needed to scrub his hands, his mind, and possibly his entire existence. As the elevator descended, the Assassin tried to focus on the task ahead. He needed to prepare for round two at the event meant to persuade voters to choose Trump to be their President. If he was successful, he'd make the choice a non-choice after all. But first, he needed a drink. Or ten. Anything to wash away the memory of what he'd just encountered.

The elevator reached the lobby, and the Assassin stepped out, blending seamlessly into the crowd of tourists and gamblers. Just another face in the sea of humanity that was Las Vegas. As he made

WRONG

his way to the nearest bar, he couldn't help but chuckle at the absurdity of it all. Here he was, a professional killer, fleeing from the sounds of flatulence and regret. Sometimes, he mused, the universe had a sick sense of humor. And tonight, it seemed, the joke was on him.

6

CARNAGE

A thousand years ago, give or take a couple centuries, a Viking warrior stood at the edge of a battlefield. Red-haired, muscle-bound, and only one neuron away from being classified as a grizzly bear, he stood at six feet tall, a tower of brute strength and primal fury. His heart thundered in his chest as he gripped his ax, staring at the enemy; raising his shield as a trumpet blew, he roared and charged forward, ready to carve his name into the annals of history with blood and steel.

Skip a thousand years, and Donald Trump was doing the same: charging toward the bathroom with a heroic brow, except his heroic battle cry sounded something more like a walrus wooing a mate. His face, normally set in that smug, defiant scowl, was now a mask of sheer panic as he

WRONG barreled down the hallway of his suite. The room's sprawling layout, which our hero previously admired for its ridiculous number of mirrors, now seemed like a cruel joke played by an architect with a sadistic streak. The bathroom felt miles away for a man on the edge of a digestive fruit-induced explosive disaster.

Finally, he saw it—the porcelain promised land, gleaming under the harsh hotel lights like a beacon of hope. With a grunting push that would have made a sumo wrestler proud, he charged ahead. The ivory doors clapped open as our pale protagonist barreled through, slamming the doors shut behind him with enough force to rattle the gold-plated fixtures. He barely made it to the toilet in time, and with a thud that shook the porcelain throne, he collapsed like a toppled statue, a monument to poor dietary choices and even poorer judgment.

What followed could only be described as a gastrointestinal apocalypse, a biblical flood of epic proportions.

The figs that had previously caused so much drama had triggered a cleanse so unholy that the bathroom seemed to tremble in response, as if even the inanimate objects were trying to escape the onslaught. Trump clutched the sides of the toilet, knuckles whitening as a massive blockage, as though years in the making, finally relented with a sound that echoed through the room like a freight train crashing into a sewage plant.

"Good Stars," he groaned, eyes squeezed shut, as if blocking out the sight of his surroundings might somehow mitigate the horrors unfolding below. The smell that filled the room was indescribable, a noxious cloud that seemed to defy the laws of physics and decency.

As the minutes ticked by and the worst of the storm subsided, Trump panted, slumping back against the tank, a steady stream of sweat diving down his face. He now felt like a deflated balloon, all the hot air that usually filled him having found a different exit. The figs—those cursed fruits of betrayal—had left him drained, physically and emotionally.

After a moment, and wiping the tears from his eyes with the back of his hand, he reached and pushed the flush handle, his hand weak and

WRONG

trembling slightly with the effort. The simple act of flushing seemed monumental, like trying to erase a mistake of cosmic proportions.

Nothing happened.

Mr. Trump paused, confused. Flush handle meant flush happen—he was almost certain that's how washrooms worked. It was one of the few certainties he had left in this moment of crisis. He jiggled the handle experimentally, then slammed it back and forth with more force, as if sheer will could make the laws of plumbing bend to his desires. The toilet gurgled evenly in response, feeble and mocking. The water level remained stubbornly high, the murky mess he had left behind refusing to disappear, much like the consequences of his actions in the real world. "You've got to be kidding me," Trump muttered, disbelieving. His voice was a mixture of desperation and indignation, as if the toilet had personally betrayed him.
Panic was finally settling in, washing over him in waves that rivaled the tsunami he'd just unleashed. Melania and the campaign team

would be arriving any minute, and the thought of them discovering this... carnage sent a shiver down Trump's spine. Imagine the headlines! The Presidential "Trump Dumps: Candidate's Bathroom Disaster Exposed!" It would be the scandal of the century, overshadowing any policy debate or political maneuvering.

He swayed back and forth on the toilet, his thighs bare and his mind racing faster than his feet could ever hope to carry him. There was no way he could petition for help; no janitor or housekeeper would ever be given this juicy story to no doubt to be passed from household to household. The thought of someone else witnessing this scene, of becoming the laughingstock of the entire hospitality industry, was too much to bear.

Then—in a rare moment of problem-solving clarity, his eyes landed on the clear trash liner folded over the top of the small wastebasket. Inspiration struck; he knew what must be done to never have to face the risk of this carnage left for the discovery from anyone else. The realization of what must be done hit Big Don with the mental equivalent of a sledgehammer.

WRONG

With a grimace that could curdle milk, Trump pulled the trash liner out of the bin, his hands trembling slightly as he stretched it out over his hand, well, just fingers really. It was a maneuver that could have been mistaken for someone handling a radioactive waste bag, except this was far worse in his mind. The thin plastic felt woefully inadequate for the task at hand, but it was all he had.

The philosopher Friedrich Nietzsche once said that he who stares into the void must know that our protagonist had never heard of Nietzsche and had no idea how to pronounce his name, as looked into the porcelain bowl, Trump felt an unmistakable horror in the pit of his stomach. He was sure that the toilet was staring back at him. It had claimed his dignity, and now...now, he had to reclaim it.

With a deep breath that he instantly regretted taking, he plunged his hand into the bowl, scooping up the unholy amalgamation of feces, wads of tissue and fig bits like a man facing his own mortality. He worked quickly, the urgency of the situation driving him forward, each scoop bringing him closer to salvation—or at least to not becoming a viral sensation for all the wrong reasons.

Just as he was finishing, a loud bang on the door startled him so badly he almost dropped the bag back into the toilet. His heart leaped into his throat, threatening to join the exodus from his body. "Room service!" called out a bored voice, followed by more knocks.

"No! No, no!" Trump yelped, his voice rising to a squeal that would have made a pig blush. Panic clawed at his throat as he plopped back onto the toilet seat, clutching the bagged abomination to his chest as if it were a ticking time bomb. In that moment, the leader of the free world was reduced to a man desperately trying to hide the evidence of his own humanity.

There was a moment of silence, one that stretched out for what felt like an eternity. But then, mercifully, the footsteps outside faded away. The threat had passed, leaving him alone

WRONG

with his shame and a bag of wet, pulpy tissue, bits of undigested fig and shit.

Exhaling in relief, Trump gingerly placed the bag on the bathroom floor, His mind raced with possibilities for disposal. He'd have to sneak it out later, somehow—maybe in a laundry bag, or stuffed into one of those complimentary bathrobes. For once, this was one problem he'd have to take care of himself, but that was a problem for future Donald.

Just as he was about to leave, he heard a knock. His heart skipped a beat, his veins growing cold—only one presence could have that effect on him.

Melania.

"Donald! Where are you?" she demanded, her accented voice cutting through his panic like a knife.

Click, click...her heels clacked against the tiles as she neared the bathroom. Then a knock sounded on the bathroom door. Melania's voice, bored and remarkably distant sounding, filtered through the wood.

Pouli Vox

"It's time to go, Donald!"

For a split second, Trump considered telling her everything—the figs, the toilet, the bag on the floor. But the thought of her icy gaze and the inevitable lecture about diet and public image made him shove that idea aside. Instead, he plastered on his most confident smile, the one he used when closing deals and facing prosecutors, and swung open the bathroom door, leaving the musk that still hung in the air behind him.

Without a second thought—or a hand wash—the presidential candidate grabbed his suit jacket from its hook, and strode out of the suite with a knightly shuffle. He was Donald Trump, after all. He'd faced worse challenges than this. Or so he told himself as they made their way to the elevator, the evidence of his ordeal safely hidden behind the bathroom door.

They walked toward the elevator in silence, Melania's face a mask of practiced indifference. As they stepped in, Trump couldn't help but feel a surge of pride. He'd handled the situation—maybe not with grace, maybe not with dignity,

WRONG

maybe not even with basic competence...but he'd handled it. After all, what was a little fruit vs bowel induced crisis to a man on the way to the oval office?

His smug smirk widened as he caught his reflection in the elevator's mirrored walls. The nightmare was over, and he was back in control— or at least, that's what he told himself as the elevator descended, taking him away from the suite, the figs, and- the bag. Little did he know, this was just the beginning of a night that would go down in history, though perhaps not in the way he imagined.

As the elevator doors closed, sealing them in, Trump stood tall, his chin jutted out in defiance of the universe itself. He was ready to face whatever the evening might bring, blissfully unaware that fate, much like his digestive system, had plans of its own.

7

THREE KILLERS, ONE TARGET

The Heart Attack Café prided itself on serving cardiac arrest with a side of fries. But right now, nestled within its sticky red walls, three entirely unaffiliated people were currently gnawing on the idea of three entirely different kinds of murderous plots to befall the man currently en route to the cafe.

The first was Sam, who had entered twenty minutes earlier and now prowled the dining room like the panther that they were becoming obsessed with after their encounter with Melania. They knew this quest was going to take stealth and perfect timing. Every step needed to be deliberate, every glance calculated. Their suit, cut so sharp it could slice through the layer of calories, cunningly hanging in the air, hugged their athletic frame in all the right places. Dark hair slicked back with enough effort to grace the

WRONG

cover of Vogue; Sam exuded an aura of effortless sophistication that seemed wildly out of place in this temple to culinary excess.

Sam's eyes scanned the room, searching for one person: Melania Trump. "She's got to be here somewhere," they muttered under their breath, a predator seeking its prey. Their gaze swept over the gaudy decor, past the waitresses in their risqué nurse outfits, and through the sea of red MAGA hats. "And once I free her from that spray-tanned sasquatch, she'll realize I'm her golden ticket out of her duties to the would-be president."

The thought of Melania alone, trapped in the undoubtedly annoying world of her shuffling oaf of a husband, stirred something deep within Sam. That feeling of rage clashed deeply and occasionally made out with an entirely different feeling that they felt toward Melania herself, which felt warm and bright and somewhat loin-stirring.

Was that love? Sam wondered. They weren't lovey-dovey,

but...perhaps. Sam managed a small smile to

typically   one   for   being

75

themselves; after a lifetime of cultivated disinterest, all these new feelings were pretty exciting.

In their pocket, a small vial of colorless, odorless poison waited. One drop in Trump's drink, and Melania would be free. It was almost poetic, really. Sam imagined themselves as a modern-day knight, slaying the fumbling, inept dragon to rescue the damsel in distress. The fact that said damsel was a grown woman who had willingly married said dragon was a minor detail Sam chose to overlook. Meanwhile, in the kitchen, Vic

was having a little
crisis. A better man might have been wrestling with the idea of killing a man, contemplating the morality of murder, and considering whether it was really worth it to get on a newsreel... Vic was

not this man. As Nico stared at him from the

corner of his eye,
Vic looked away innocently as he meandered around the kitchen, narrowly dodging line cooks and waiters as they charged past him. His eyes darted to the back door, leading to the alley.

WRONG

That's where he'd do it. Lure Trump out for a "private chat about campaign contributions," then introduce his larynx to Vic's hands that had a surprisingly strong grip after his many years of his attempts at anger suppression. Simple, effective, and best of all, it would keep the mess out of his kitchen.

Inside Vic's greasy little noggin, the thought process was simple. If he took out Trump, he'd be a hero. Or maybe a villain. But he'd definitely be on CNN. His face would be plastered across every news channel, his name on everyone's lips. He'd be infamous, remembered forever as the man who changed the course of history. The fact that this infamy would likely come with a life sentence was a detail Vic's mind conveniently skipped over.

Even as the goatee-afflicted manager grappled with his escape plan—or lack thereof—the Assassin shuffled into the Heart Attack, looking less like a hired killer and more like a disgruntled substitute teacher who'd been roped into babysitting a class of unruly kids. He grimaced as his joints protested, a painful reminder of why he should've retired years ago.

Pouli Vox

He hadn't been able to finish the target off at the suite, and he still looked mildly traumatized from the...noises he had heard emanating from it, even after two stiff martinis. But now, armed with a ~~silenced pistol and~~ renewed sense of a desperation, he was ready to try again. His plan was simple: wait for the right moment, sidle up behind Trump, and introduce the back of his head to a small piece of lead traveling at high velocity. Quick, quiet, and hopefully effective.

The Assassin sighed, remembering Jeffrey's words: "You owe me, old man. One last job, and we're square." He'd been stupid enough to bet his life savings on some hot stock tip from a guy who looked like he ate insider trading for breakfast. Now, thanks to a toxic mixture of his bad judgment and Boeing trades here he was, about to potentially murder a presidential candidate just to clear his debt. Life had a sick sense of humor.

The dining area of the restaurant was a cacophony of sights, sounds, and smells that assaulted the senses like a mugging in a dark alley. The walls, painted a shade of red usually

WRONG

reserved for fire trucks and mid-life crisis sports cars, were adorned with posters glorifying the virtues of cholesterol and saturated fats. Neon signs flickered and buzzed, casting an eerie glow over the sea of red MAGA hats that filled the booths.

Waitresses, dressed in "nurse" uniforms that seemed to have shrunk in the wash, navigated the crowded floor with trays piled high with artery-clogging delights. Their outfits, more suitable for a bachelor party than a medical facility, left little to the imagination. Both men and women alike ogled shamelessly as they passed, eyes following the sway of hips and the bounce of barely contained assets.

The air was thick with the smell of burning grease, sweaty bodies, and the faint hint of desperation. Conversations overlapped, creating an aura that was part rowdy sports bar, part political rally, and part food fight at a preschool for adults.

"I'm telling you, Keith, this Trump guys got the right idea," a portly bald man in an ill-fitting suit bellowed to his companion, bits of half-chewed burger spraying from his mouth. "We need someone who knows how to make deals. Real deals, you know?"

His friend, nursing what appeared to be his third confidence shot in a glass, nodded sagely.
"Damn straight. Did you hear about that golf course deal he pulled off in Scotland? Pure genius. Who cares about some stupid protected wetlands when you can have eighteen holes of pure golfing paradise?"

At another table, a group of men in expensive suits and cheap toupees huddled together, speaking in hushed tones that somehow still carried over the din.
"Listen, if Trump gets in, we're golden," one whispered, his eyes darting around nervously. "I've got it on good authority that he's planning to gut the EPA. Think of the possibilities!"
His companion grinned, revealing teeth stained by years of cigar smoke and moral decay. "I hear you. I've got a couple hundred acres of 'worthless' land that'll suddenly become prime real estate species

once those pesky endangered regulations are out of the way."

WRONG

They all chuckled, the sound reminiscent of hyenas circling a wounded gazelle.

As Trump's arrival was announced, the three would-be killers perked up like meerkats spotting a juicy grub. Sam's eyes locked onto Melania, their heart doing a little salsa number. Vic's hand tightened around an imaginary neck, his goatee quivering with anticipation. The Assassin's fingers ghosted over the hidden weapon in his coat, a grimace of determination etched on his face. Trump sauntered in, looking like a Muppet

that
had been stuffed into a suit that was at least a size too small. Melania followed her face frozen in a mask of elitism that would make a statue jealous. The crowd cheered, the cameras flashed, and our three anti-heroes prepared to make their life-changing, and possibly even ending moves.
Sam edged closer, vial of poison at the ready, rehearsing their "Melania, I'm your knight in shining Armani" speech. Vic shuffled towards the back door, ready to lure Trump into his trap. The

Pouli Vox

~~Assa~~ssin stalked forward, trying to inconspicuous while maneuvering for a clear shot.

And then, because the universe has a twisted sense of humor, chaos suddenly erupts.
Vic, in his haste to shake hands with Trump, slipped on a puddle of spilled Diet Coke, that, atop the greasy floor made for an extra slippery lubricant and he and went sliding across the floor like a penguin on an ice rink. He collided with Sam, who had been mid-stride in their attempt to get close enough to spike Trump's drink. The two of them careened into the Assassin, who had been adjusting his aim.

The result was a spectacular pile-up of failed assassins, looking less like a coordinated attack and more like a Three Stooges routine gone horribly wrong. Sam's perfect hair was mussed, their vial of poison now empty beneath them. Vic's apron had somehow ended up over his head and wrapped awkwardly around his body, his dreams of strangulation glory dashed. The Assassin lay flat on his back, his silencer bent at

WRONG

an angle that suggested it would be more likely to curve a bullet around Trump than actually hit him.

"Let me guess," the Assassin managed, his voice worthless

a pained whisper, "You...two idiots...were gunning for him too?" "Why else

would I be here," said Sam, nose wrinkled as they sat up and inspected the state of their ruined suit. "I would only follow my love".

Vic, meanwhile, was very obviously sulking. "This was supposed to be my moment. My chance to save America from that walking Cheeto."

"It was my chance to rid Melania of that sour bastard," Sam muttered.
The Assassin sighed. "It was my chance to afford my next mortgage payment."
Together, they turned to look at Trump's table.

He
continued his onion ring feast as he waited for his burger, entirely oblivious to the fact that he'd just narrowly avoided being assassinated by three entirely different people. The trio of would-be killers in question, meanwhile, continued to sit

there in a pile of bruised egos and even more bruised bodies, wondering how it all went so spectacularly wrong.

As they watched, a waitress approached Trump's table with a massive milkshake, could it have gotten poisoned after all? The waitress, possibly purchased having to counter-balance her breasts, nearly tripped over her own feet. The three failed assassins held their breath, hoping for some divine intervention. But Trump, in a rare moment of grace, knocked the glass over before it reached his lips. The milkshake pooled around his feet, looking suspiciously like the dreams of our hapless trio.

Sam, Vic, and the Assassin exchanged glances, a silent acknowledgment passing between them. They'd failed spectacularly, but at least they weren't alone in their failure. And really, wasn't that what life was all about? Finding kindred spirits in the depths of your own incompetence? Trying to make any silver lining from their failure felt absurd.

As security started to take notice of their little huddle, the three scrambled to their feet, ready to

WRONG

make hasty exits. They may have failed in their missions, but they'd succeeded in creating a bond forged in the fires of shared humiliation. And isn't that, in its own way, a kind of victory?

(Spoiler alert: It's not.)

As they slunk away, each nursing their wounds and bruised egos, they couldn't help but wonder what twist of fate had brought them together in this moment of spectacular failure. Little did they know, the night was far from over, and destiny had a few more surprises in store for them all.

8

CHEW

The fundraiser was still in full swing, a grotesque tableau of excess and self-interest that would have made even the most tyrannical emperor blush. The Heart Attack Café buzzed with the feverish energy of loud, obnoxious tycoon types that only obscene wealth and unchecked ambition could generate. Slick politicians whose smiles never quite reached 100% authenticity due to their closeness to calculating eyes mingled with the crowd, their laughter a touch too loud, their handshakes a bit too firm.

Waitresses in their provocative nurse uniforms navigated the chaos like ships through the treacherous waters, some merely enduring their shifts with gritted teeth, others eyeing a chance at viral fame or dreaming of a Melania-esque ascent up the gilded social ladder. The air was thick with

WRONG

the smell of grease, perfume, and the unmistakable scent of desperation.

At the epicenter of this maelstrom of greed and gluttony sat Donald Trump, a bloated sun around which these lesser planets frantically orbited. Ensconced in his semi-private VIP booth, he projected an air of a kingpin holding court. He wanted to be admired from afar, but ultimately left undisturbed.

Those who approached him did so deferentially, addressing him in a "Godfather-esque" manner, seeking favors and requests to be granted. They bowed and scraped, their eyes gleaming with a mixture of hope and fear, as if approaching a temperamental deity who might bless them or strike them down on a whim.

His signature coif, defying both gravity and good taste, gleamed under the gaudy chandeliers. He nodded and grinned, a plastered-on rictus of self-satisfaction, agreeing to every deal presented with a booming "Absolutely!" or a conspiratorial wink. In the recesses of his mind, he knew full well he'd either forget or disregard half of these promises later. It didn't matter; these people took things far too seriously anyway. They were all just pawns in his grand game of ego gratification.

A union rep, his suit straining against the pressure of too many steakhouse dinners, sidled up to Trump. His voice oozed with the kind of sycophantic charm that comes from years of greasing palms and massaging egos. "Mr. President," he drawled, winking obviously and leaning in close enough for Trump to smell the whiskey on his breath, "we've got a little token of our appreciation. A custom Tesla truck with your face splattered all over the paint job- your fans will love it. Gold-plated everything, sir. Even the damn tires."

Trump's eyes lit up like a child promised the keys to a candy store. "Sounds tremendous," he boomed, slapping the man on the back hard enough to make him wince. "The best car. Everyone will be jealous, believe me. We'll drive it right down Pennsylvania Avenue, show those losers what a real President looks like!" But even as he nodded along to the union rep's fawning description of the car's features, Trump's true focus was divided between two things: the

WRONG

massive cheeseburger being brought his way on a silver platter and the young waitresses flitting about the room. His gaze followed one particular girl, barely out of her teens, as she giggled at some crude joke from a red-faced senator.

Trump leaned in close to a nearby donor, his breath hot and fetid. "How old do you think these girls are?" he asked, a lascivious grin spreading across his face. Before the man could stammer out a response, Trump chuckled and added, "Do they have any younger?"

The donor's laughter, a sound like gravel in a blender, was mercifully drowned out by the arrival of Trump's heart-stopping feast. The burger was a monstrosity, a towering edifice of beef, cheese, and every manner of fried accoutrement imaginable. It arrived on a platter larger than some of the waitresses' torsos, surrounded by a moat of overdone fries glistening with grease and salt.

Trump's eyes widened at the sight, his pupils dilating with an almost orgasmic pleasure. He'd flown to Vegas for this, yes, under the guise of a fundraiser, but this is what really got his blood pumping. He dismissed the would-be bootlicker and seized the burger with both hands, grease already dribbling down his chin as he took a massive bite. The room continued its drunken dance around him, a cacophony of deals being struck, insults being hurled, and waitresses playfully spanking the more boisterous guests with novelty paddles emblazoned with the café's logo.

Trump barely registered the chatter swirling around him.
"We can get those zoning laws changed by next week..."
"Did you see the rack on that one? I'd have a meeting with them all night long!"
"Ten million? Child's play. We can double that by Tuesday..."
He was too busy forcing down another massive chunk of beef and cheese, barely chewing in his gluttonous frenzy. His face was flushed, sweat beading on his forehead from the effort of consuming such a monstrous creation. And then, mid-bite, as he opened his mouth to catcall the passing waitress he'd had his eye on when it happened:

WRONG

The mass of half-chewed burger lodged firmly in his throat.

For a moment, Trump didn't even realize what was happening. He tried to swallow. The amalgam of cheese and beef and bun was mostly, but certainly not all the way down and through his throat, and it refused to budge. Panic began to set in as he realized he couldn't breathe. His eyes bulged, bloodshot and terrified. He tried to cough, to speak, but nothing came out save for a weak, wheezing gasp. The deal-making and debauchery continued
around him, oblivious to his distress. Trump, still silenced, but gasping for air through the burger, made a flitty back hand motion to a donor nearby who merely said, "Pardon me," before turning back to his conversation about offshore accounts and shell companies. Trump's face began to turn an alarming shade of
blue, clashing horribly with his pale, mottled skin. His vision started to swim, the room becoming a blur of color and noise. He tried again to grab someone, anyone, but his arms felt like lead

weights. His legs gave way, and he discreetly slumped back into the grimy, vinyl upholstered booth, his head only slightly bobbed to one side, Weekend at Bernies style.

For a moment, the chaos continued unabated. Glasses clinked, laughter roared, and in the back of the room at a private table, Melania sat, unengaged and on her phone, continuing to "add to cart". Then, a single voice cut through the din:

"Oh my God, Donald!" Just then as heads turned,

the room finally and
collectively registered the THUD as Trump's body finally gave way to gravity and slid onto the floor, sprawled out, face pressed against the filthy tiles, still slightly gasping like a fish out of water. His hands flailed weakly, fingers scrabbling at his throat in a futile attempt to dislodge the obstruction.

The room paused for a heartbeat; an eternity compressed into a single moment of shocked silence. In that instant, a hundred calculations were made behind a hundred pairs of eyes. Save the man who promised them the world, or let

WRONG

nature take its course? In that moment of hesitation, as Trump's vision began to darken and his movements became more frantic, it became clear that to most in the room, he was merely a means to an end – and there were plenty of other ends to pursue.

A few pulled out their phones, not to call for help, but to capture what might be a viral moment. The question hung in the air, unanswered: Had anyone noticed in time?

As Trump's consciousness began to fade, his life flashing before his eyes in a parade of gold-plated toilets and ill-fitting suits, he had one final, bitter realization. In a room full of people who had sworn loyalty to him, who had promised him the world, not a single hand was reaching out to save him.

The last thing Donald Trump saw before the darkness claimed him was his own reflection in a nearby mirror, blue-faced and undignified, sprawled on the floor of a tacky themed restaurant. It was, perhaps, a fitting end for a man who had lived his life in pursuit of spectacle, disruption and excess.

Pouli Vox

The Café fell silent, the only sound the wet gasps of a dying man and the soft click of camera phones capturing his final moments. Outside, oblivious to the drama unfolding within, a neon sign flickered: "Eat here and beat the odds!"

For Donald Trump, the odds had finally caught up.

9

WRONG

After the few vital moments, The Heart Attack Café descended into chaos as Donald Trump lay motionless on the grease-slicked floor, his face an alarming shade of blue that clashed horribly with the garish decor. The cacophony of deal-making and sleazy jokes gave way to a stunned silence, punctuated only by the occasional gasp or nervous whisper. The room smelled of fear, confusion, and deep-fried everything.

Our three would-be assassins – Sam, Victory, and the Assassin – found themselves drawn together in the crowd, united by their shared goal and mutual confusion. They stood in a small circle, eyeing each other suspiciously, each wondering if one of the others had somehow succeeded where they had failed.

Pouli Vox

It was a question that gnawed at all three of them. Trump, the man who had been the target of their wildly differing and increasingly convoluted plans, was now lying on the floor without needing a single moment of their help, his hands spread flat like tiny pancakes, his nose squished against the floor like one of his favorite overripe figs. The question in their minds was simple: Who could have killed the man everyone wanted dead?

"Russians?" Vic hazarded, his voice barely above a whisper, eyes darting around nervously.
"Nope, best buds," the Assassin replied, his tone dry and matter-of-fact. "Maybe communists?"
"Too broke," Sam said, their eyes never leaving the prone figure of Trump. "Another hitman?"
"No one else was taking the job, pays like shit," the Assassin shrugged, wincing slightly as his joints protested. "Then who could have done

this?" Vic asked, in a
tone that was meant to be dramatic but failed entirely, coming across more like a whiny child denied dessert.

WRONG

Sam looked at the Assassin with clear accusation. "I didn't even get a chance to spike his milkshake, and you didn't even let me try and save him."

"And you need to make up your mind," said the Assassin, his voice tinged with exasperation. "I'd have had fewer witnesses, and you two would be dead, for starters."

"Hm," said Sam absently, watching as the paramedics barged into the diner, pushing

Through the rubbernecking crowd. waitresses, who had spent the last hour slinging triple bypass burgers and dodging the lewd comments of ranchers in ten-gallon hats, were positively delighted by this—after all, if there's one thing a gal in uniform loves, it's someone in an entirely different uniform. Sam counted at least three paramedics who would definitely be getting lucky later.

They sighed, pulling away the stubborn fry from their suit. "This wasn't supposed to happen. I had a whole speech prepared for later," they muttered, sounding almost hurt. "Something about freeing her from her gilded cage. It was very poetic."

Sam, still picking cheese fries off of their designer suit, whispered, "Did... did we do this?" Their voice quivered with a mix of hope and dread, like a child who's just realized they might have wished too hard for a snow day. Vic, his apron stained with various condiments that formed a Jackson Pollock of fast-food art, shook his head in disappointment. "I didn't even get a chance to spike that milkshake," he muttered, his eyes darting nervously around the room. "I was waiting for him to order the 'Trump Tower of Dairy' special."

Chet, the Assassin, rubbing his aching joints, grumbled, "If I'd done it, there'd be more... pizzazz. And fewer witnesses." As paramedics rushed in, pushing through the the crowd of gawking onlookers with determination of salmon swimming upstream, our trio of failed eliminators grappled with a cocktail of emotions more complex than the café's secret sauce recipe.

WRONG

Sam felt a twinge of disappointment mixed with relief, like finding out your flight's been canceled right after you've rushed to the airport. Their elaborate plan to seduce Melania away from Trump's cold, spray-tanned hands had been thwarted by... what exactly? "I had a whole speech prepared," they muttered again, "I even learned how to say 'You deserve better' in Slovenian."

The Manager's mind raced with opportunities and sudden fear. He'd spent weeks agonizing over whether to go through with his plan, and now... this? "I could've been famous," he lamented, wringing his hands. "Or infamous. Either way, I'd have gotten a book deal. But what if they think I did this? Oh man, what if I get blamed for something I didn't even have the guts to do?"

The Assassin, meanwhile, found himself oddly nostalgic and suspicious. "Back in my day," he began, before catching himself. "Geez, I really am turning into my father. Next thing you know, I'll be complaining about the price of piano wire." He squinted at the chaotic scene. "But seriously, who beat us to the punch? This feels... amateur hour. Where's the style? The panache?"

The initial shock gave way to a disturbing pragmatism that spread through the room like a virus of opportunism. "Say," a Texas oil baron drawled, his voice cutting through the tension like a hot knife through butter, "if he doesn't make it, does that mean our deals are off? Cause I've got some prime real estate I was hoping to offload."

A politician in a suit that screamed "discount rack at Men's Wearhouse" chimed in, his eyes gleaming with barely concealed excitement, "I've got my dibs on his voter base! I've been practicing 'tremendous' and 'believe me' in the mirror for months!"

"Dibs on the golden toilet!" someone shouted from the back, their voice filled with a disturbing amount of enthusiasm for used bathroom fixtures.

Our trio watched in disgusted fascination as the very people who'd been fawning over Trump

WRONG

moments ago now circled like vultures, ready to pick his empire clean before his body had even cooled. It was a stark reminder of the transient nature of power and loyalty in their world.

"Is this what we wanted?" Sam wondered aloud; their voice barely audible over the growing frenzy. "To unleash... this?" They gestured at the throng of opportunists, now practically salivating at the prospect of carving up Trump's legacy.

The Manager nodded slowly, his earlier panic giving way to a sort of philosophical resignation. "It's like they say: be careful what you wish for. You just might get it... and then realize it comes with a side of existential dread and possible legal repercussions."

"Who says that?" the Assassin grumbled, his brow furrowed. "Sounds like something my mother would say. Oh god, it's happening again. Next thing you know, I'll be telling kids to get off my lawn and complaining about how music these days is just noise."

Sam, Vic, and the Assassin found themselves caught between relief and paranoia. Had one of them succeeded without realizing it? Was there another player in this deadly game they hadn't accounted for?

"Maybe it was just... natural causes?" Vic suggested weakly, his voice tinged with hope and disbelief in equal measure.

Sam scoffed, the sound dripping with sarcasm. "Natural? In this place? The only thing natural here is the rate at which it clogs arteries. Even the air feels like it's 90% cheese particles."

The Assassin squinted suspiciously at the crowd, his professional paranoia kicking into high gear. "I don't like it. It's too... convenient. In my line of work, convenience usually means someone else got there first. Or that you're about to walk into a trap. Or both. Usually both."

"Well," Sam sighed, looking around the room trying to catch Melania's eye, "I guess we'll have to wait to find out what really happened. Just like everyone else. How... ordinary."

"Or," Vic suggested, a glimmer of his old scheming self-returning, "one of us could just

WRONG

take the credit for whatever did just happen, whatever it was seemed to have worked better than our plans."

The Assassin nodded sagely, stroking his chin in a way that he hoped made him look wise and not like he was checking for missed stubble. The three began to conspire. Surely, they could concoct a story that would read plausible to Jeffrey for the Assassin to report, heroic to Melania for Sam's benefit and a sensational, inspiring story for the media that would ensure Vic's fame and fortune, but they'd have to act fast, the new plot unable to fail.

Little did they realize, their harrowing ordeal and the enigma surrounding the true events were far from resolution. The cosmos, it seemed, possessed an innate yearning for justice and scant patience for would-be martyrs and subterfuge. The universe has a darker sense of humor than any assassin could ever devise. And sometimes a cheeseburger might succeed where elaborate plots fail. In such cases, the universe may dispatch an emissary - in this instance, an angel of truth.

Pouli Vox

As our trio huddled together, plotting their next move, they remained blissfully unaware that their carefully constructed narratives were about to be unraveled by an unexpected arrival. The truth, it seemed, was about to make its grand entrance, and it wore a Hawaiian shirt.

10

MUNGER

As the chaos at the Heart Attack Café had begun to settle as the party was clearly over, an unexpected figure wandered through the door, parting the sea of panicked onlookers like an easy-going Moses. Dr. E. Munger, a visiting coroner, sported a shirt so loud it almost drowned out the panicked voices around him. Palm trees and flamingos danced across his belly, that only seemed to amplify his good nature creating a mesmerizing optical illusion with each step. His walrus mustache twitched with barely contained excitement, like a caterpillar doing the cha-cha on his upper lip. "Well, call me Sassy!" he exclaimed, taking in the scene with the glee of a kid in a candy store. "And here I thought the zip line would be the most thrilling part of my vacation! Shows what I know about Sin City!"

The café, now a makeshift crime scene, buzzed with tension. Yellow tape crisscrossed the entrance like a macabre Christmas decoration, and shell-shocked diners huddled in booths, clutching their Triple Bypass Burgers like life preservers. The air was thick with the smell of grease, fear, and the faint metallic tang of mortality.

Munger approached the sheet-covered body on the floor, humming "Viva Las Vegas" under his breath. He knelt down with a grunt that sounded suspiciously like "Oof, too many cheeseburgers," followed by a muttered, "Note to self: lay off the all-you-can-eat buffets" and chuckled to himself at the joke. "Let's see what we've got here," he muttered, pulling back the sheet with the flourish of a magician revealing his final trick. "Oh my, if it isn't the man himself. Well, sir, I bet you never thought you'd actually meet your maker in a place called the Heart Attack Café. Life's funny that way, isn't it? One minute you're on top of the world, the next

WRONG

you're face-down in a pile of cheese fries. A modern tragedy, really."

As Munger examined the body, our trio inched closer, straining to hear any clues about their potential involvement. They looked like guilty dogs trying to sneak past their owner after raiding the trash, all shifty eyes and nervous energy.

After what seemed like an eternity filled with "Hmms," "Ahas," and one particularly loud "Well, I'll be a monkey's uncle!" Munger stood up, his knees popping louder than Alyssa Edwards. "Alright, folks," he announced, his jolly demeanor at odds with the somber mood, like a clown at a funeral. "I've seen enough to make a preliminary determination. Now, I'm just a simple country coroner, but I've seen my fair share of unusual deaths. Why, this one time in Reno—"

"The cause of death, Doctor?" an impatient detective interrupted, his voice tight with the strain of a man who'd seen too much weird shit for one day.

"Oh, right, right," Munger chuckled, his belly jiggling like a bowl full of jelly. "Sorry, I do tend to ramble. Occupational hazard when most of your clients can't tell you to shut up. Well, it appears our esteemed almost-president here has given us all a very important lesson. And that lesson is..." he paused for dramatic effect, his mustache quivering with anticipation, "always chew your food thoroughly!"

A collective gasp rippled through the crowd, followed by a few confused murmurs and one person in the back asking, "Wait, is this a PSA about choking? I thought we were here for a crime scene." "Are you saying..." the detective began,

his face a

mask of disbelief.

"Yep," Munger nodded, his mustache bouncing merrily like it was doing a little dance of its own. "Choked on a cheeseburger. A real whopper of a burger, if you'll pardon the pun. Now, I'm 99.8% certain of this – which, coincidentally, is the same percentage of saturated fat in that burger.

WRONG

As the room erupted in a cacophony of disbelief and poorly disguised relief, not poisoned? Not actually a heart attack or overdose of Viagra as many had begun to deduce? Munger continued his impromptu lecture, clearly relishing his moment in the spotlight.

As Munger expounded on the dangers of hasty eating ("It's not a race, folks! Unless you're in a competitive eating contest, in which case, may God have mercy on your colon."), he seemed to look directly at Sam, the Manager, and the Assassin. His eyes twinkled with a knowing gleam that made them squirm like kids caught with their hands in the cookie jar.

"You know," he said, his voice dropping conspiratorially, "The universe, folks, has some pretty simple rules. Chew your food. Don't talk with your mouth full. Treat others with kindness. Tip your waitstaff. Mr. Trump, in his haste to make deals and crack inappropriate jokes, forgot these fundamental truths. And the consequences, as we can see, were dire. And greasy. Very, very greasy."

Pouli Vox

The room was silent now, hanging on his every word like laundry on a clothesline.

"The moral of the story, my friends, is this: No one is above the rules. Not you, not me, and certainly not the President – or almost-President – of the United States. All the elaborate assassination attempts in the world couldn't touch him, but a simple cheeseburger and a failure to follow basic table manners? That was his undoing. It's like my dear old grandpop used to say: 'You can run from the law, you can run from your ex-wife, but you can't run from a poorly chewed bite of beef.'" again, Munger looked pleased at his impromptu joke.

"Sometimes the universe has a way of course-correcting all on its own. No need for elaborate plans or schemes. Just a twist of fate... or in this case, a twist of burger. It's almost like the cosmos has a sense of humor, isn't it? And let me tell you, after years in this job, I've learned that if you don't laugh, you'll cry. And crying is terrible for digestion."

Our trio of failed assassins exchanged glances of bewilderment. All their elaborate plans, and in

WRONG

the end, it was a simple hunk of meat that did the job? It was like finding out Goliath had been felled not by David's sling, but by a particularly aggressive hangnail.

With a glance in their direction that left them wondering if he somehow knew about their failed attempts, Munger made his way towards the exit, his Hawaiian shirt a riot of color in the subdued crime scene.

"Well, I'm off to that zip line," he announced to no one in particular. "After all, what's the point of a Vegas vacation if you don't dance with the devil once in a while? Might as well enjoy it while we can! But remember, kids: chew your food, look both ways before crossing, be kind to the wait staff and never, ever run with scissors! Oh, and maybe consider a salad once in a while. Your arteries will thank you and you never know when the universe might be keeping score."

With a wink and a nod, Munger slowly saunters towards the exit, leaving behind a room full of people with a lot to digest – both literally and figuratively.

11

THE RESULTS ARE IN

Melania Trump was only now realizing that something was amiss with her husband. While Donald had been turning blue and causing a commotion, she had been engrossed in a conversation with a group of socialites discussing the latest fashion trends and the merits of various European getaways. The constant din of the café, combined with her practiced ability to tune out her husband's frequent outbursts, had rendered her blissfully unaware of the unfolding drama.

"Donald?" she called out, her voice a mixture of annoyance and dawning concern. "What is this commotion? Her accent, usually carefully subdued, became more pronounced in her irritation.

WRONG

As she made her way through the throng of onlookers, realization slowly dawned on her face. Her expression shifted from mild irritation to confusion, then to shock, and finally settled on a complex mixture of emotions that even she couldn't quite define. It was as if her face was struggling to decide between relief, horror, and the sudden realization that her life was about to change dramatically.

"Oh," she said simply, as the full weight of the situation finally hit her. "I see."

For a moment, she stood there, seemingly unsure of how to react. Then, with the poise of someone who had weathered many public storms, she straightened her designer jacket, cleared her throat, and addressed the nearest person who looked official.

"I suppose we'll need to reschedule the rest of this week's events," she said, her voice steady and controlled. "And I'll need to speak with our lawyer."

Pouli Vox

Clearing her throat with a sound not unlike a car trying to start on a cold morning, Melania tried to disguise her belated realization...the realization that her husband fell victim to something far more powerful than any poison, plot, or political maneuvering. He fell victim to hubris, and perhaps more literally, to his own insatiable appetite.

As the neon lights of Las Vegas continued their relentless dance outside, the Heart Attack Café stood as a monument to irony. Inside, the chaos had settled into a stunned quiet, punctuated only by the occasional flash of a camera or the hushed whispers of disbelief.

Donald Trump, the man who had seemed larger than life, who had weathered scandals and controversies with the resilience of a cockroach, had finally met his match in the form of a cheeseburger. The universe, it seemed, had a twisted sense of humor, and somewhere, in the great beyond, Donald Trump was undoubtedly demanding to speak to the manager about the most unfair results of his circumstance.

WRONG

As the paramedics finally managed to load Trump's body onto a stretcher, Sam, Vic, and the Assassin found themselves huddled in a corner, still processing the bizarre turn of events.

"Well," Sam said, breaking the silence, "I suppose this means I won't be needing that Cartier panther after all." They glanced wistfully at Melania, who was now speaking in hushed tones with a group of advisors.

Vic, his dreams of infamy shattered, looked utterly deflated. "What am I supposed to do now? Go back to managing a restaurant where the main attraction just killed a presidential candidate?"

The Assassin, meanwhile, was eyeing the exits. "I don't know about you two, but I'm thinking early retirement might be in order. I hear Belize is nice this time of year."

As they contemplated their next moves, Dr. Munger's words echoed in their minds. Perhaps the universe did have a way of correcting itself, of meting out justice in the most unexpected ways.

Pouli Vox

Melania, now surrounded by a phalanx of security and advisors, cast one last look around the restaurant. Her eyes met Sam's for a brief moment, and something passed between them – a hint of what might have been, perhaps. But then she turned away, her face once again a mask of cool detachment.

As the crowd began to disperse and the reality of what had transpired settled in, our trio of failed assassins realized that their paths, so briefly intertwined, were about to diverge once more. Sam straightened their suit, a hint of their old confidence returning. "Well, gentleman, it's been... an experience. I think I'll take this as a sign to pursue less complicated romantic entanglements." Vic nodded glumly. "I suppose I

should go see
about getting the 'Trump Tower Burger' off the menu. Might be in poor taste now." The Assassin

chuckled, wincing as he stretched
his aching joints. "And I've got a rather awkward phone call to make to a certain employer. Somehow, I don't think 'the target choked on a

WRONG

burger before I could get to him' is going to fly as an excuse."

As they prepared to go their separate ways, each contemplating the strange twists of fate that had brought them to this moment, they couldn't help but feel a strange sense of camaraderie. They had failed in their individual missions, yes, but they had also been witnesses to a moment of *unprecedented* historic absurdity.

EPILOGUE:

EVIDENCE

The dead man's suite was quiet.

At the Wynn, life continued as usual. No one had yet been notified about the circumstances unfolding down on Fremont Street. Tonight, like all other nights, turndown service was on its way, as had been requested several times and rather rudely by Donald Trump himself.
The staff, blissfully unaware of the evening's events, approached the presidential suite, armed with fresh towels and mints for pillows, ready to face whatever demands their highly demanding guest might make.

This evening though, there would be a discovery unlike anything else. Because more noteworthy

WRONG

than any money left behind, crass sound bites, divisiveness, or political madness, the one thing he would *truly* be remembered for was sitting inside the darkness- there on the tile, slumping, still wet, adding an unmistakable aroma to the room.

A legacy, ripe with the stench of mortality, just waiting to be discovered.

THE EMPIRE PUBLISHERS

The Empire Publishers publishing
12808 West Airport Blvd Suite 270M Sugar Land, TX 77478
https://empirepublishers.co/about-us

Our books may be purchased in bulk for promotional, educational, or business use. Please contact The Empire Publishers at +(844) 636-4576, or by email at support@theempirepublishers.com